Fifi the footballer

Written by
Mary G Mbabazi

Illustrated by
Peter Gitego

There once lived an eight year old girl named Fifi. She liked football very much. She used to follow her brother whenever he went to play with his friends.

Fifi always wondered why girls never played football, for she had never seen a girl play.

"I should join the boys one day and play with them," she thought, "I wonder if they will allow me."

One evening at home, Fifi asked her brother, "Fred, can I join you tomorrow to play football?"

"No Fifi!" her brother answered, "My friends cannot let you play with us. But don't worry, I will teach you how to play."

"Thank you!" Fifi said excitedly.

In the days that followed, Fifi trained with her brother. They trained in the evening after doing their class homework and other chores.

After a few weeks of training, Fifi joined her brother and his friends to play.

"Girls are not allowed to play," the boys said at once when they saw Fifi.

"Why don't you allow girls to play?" Fifi asked them.

"Because girls are not strong enough to hit the ball," they answered.

"I think some girls like me can do better than you boys," Fifi said.

The boys laughed except her brother Fred.

"How can girls do better than boys?" the boys said, "Impossible!"

Then suddenly Fifi took the ball from one of the boys and started bouncing it on her knee. The boys were impressed and surprised! Her brother Fred just smiled...

"Does anyone want to go to the net?" Fifi challenged the boys.

"Sure, I will go," one of the boys known to be the best goalkeeper said.

Fifi then hit the ball and it went straight into the net.

"Goal!" she screamed. She ran around excitedly and hugged her brother.

The boys could not believe it.

"Good job Fifi!" the boys said.

"I didn't know a girl could hit a ball like that!" one of the boys said, "You should join our team."

All the boys then agreed that Fifi should join their football team.

From then, Fifi went with her brother to play football and became very good at it. During one school competition, other young girls noticed how Fifi was a good footballer.

"Fifi, can you teach us how to play?" four of her friends later asked.

"Yes, I will teach you!" Fifi responded.

She started training the girls every evening after school.

Months later, a team of strong girl players was formed. Fifi left the boys team and became the captain of the girls' team that she had created. The girls' team was so good that they won many competitions and travelled around the world.

ISBN: 978-99977-771-9-5

Email: furahapublishers@gmail.com

www.furahapublisher.com